ELLA

Diaries

TOP SECRET!

Meredith Costain

For Zac and the 'real' Lizzie, Robert, Claire and Sian,
and in memory of Harriet the Wondercat—M.C.

For my gorgeous husband, Ray.
I love you—D.M.

Danielle McDonald

First American Edition 2016
Kane Miller, A Division of EDC Publishing

Text copyright © Meredith Costain, 2015
Illustrations copyright © Danielle McDonald, 2015

First published by Scholastic Australia, a division of Scholastic Australia Pty Limited in 2015.
This edition published under license from Scholastic Australia Pty Limited.

For information contact:
Kane Miller, A Division of EDC Publishing
PO Box 470663
Tulsa, OK 74147-0663
www.kanemiller.com
www.edcpub.com
www.usbornebooksandmore.com

Library of Congress Control Number: 2015954252

Printed and bound in the United States of America

8 9 10 11 12 13 14 15

ISBN: 978-1-61067-522-2

❀ 1 ❀

ELLA
Diaries

I ♥ Pets

Kane Miller
A DIVISION OF EDC PUBLISHING

Friday, after school

Dear Diary,

You know how some days are better than others? Well, today was one of those days. It was an exceptionally excellent, outstanding, superb, very, very GOOD day.

Every year we have a Careers Day. Last year it was Special Services Day, with police and firefighters and ambulance drivers and a REAL Fire Truck.

We thought the fire truck belonged to the firefighters that came to talk to us. But then we found out the truck ~~acksherly~~ actually belonged to a DIFFERENT bunch of firefighters, who came to fight a real fire at the school. Mr. Zugaro accidentally started one in the teachers' lounge when he was showing Ms. Diablo how to make a rocket out of a tea bag.

ROCKET

Tea BAG

But for this year's Careers Day, all the people who came to talk to us were animal experts. I 🩶 animals MORE THAN ANYTHING (except maybe chocolate cake). I'm always asking Mom and Dad if we can get more pets but sadly their answer is always no.

It is BREAKING MY HEART, dear Diary.

Some of the people brought the animals
they work with to our school. I was SO
EXCITED! This is who we met:

1. Carlos (a zookeeper)
with Eric, a gigantic
Eastern tarantula from
tropical Queensland who
barks and whistles.

2. Minnie (a therapy
dog handler) with
Coco, a labradoodle
puppy.

3. Jess (a stable
groom and horse
exerciser).

4 Angus (a wildlife rehabilitator) with wally, a rescued wombat joey.

5 Effie (a herpetologist) with Charlie, a slithery snake.

WaLLY

charLiE

Zoe was really disappointed Jess didn't bring any horses with her for us to ride. Zoe is HORSE CRAZY.

ZOE

But she went all pale and trembly when she saw Charlie. Zoe is super scared of snakes, ever since she nearly stood on one by accident when she was on a family picnic in the bush and it hissed at her.

Coco, the labradoodle, was so CUTE! Minnie said we could pat her as long as we were really gentle. Of course Precious Princess Peach Parker (the most annoying, irritating, maddening, infuriating person in the history of the ~~world~~ ~~galaxy~~ universe) had to pick her up and hold on to her FOREVER so there was no time for anyone else to have a turn.

She kept telling Minnie how good she was with all animals but especially puppies, and how she wanted to be a therapy dog handler too when she grows up, and asking her all these questions like, "How old are they when they start training?" and "How long do you train them for?"

Anyone with even a tiny brain would know the answers, because Minnie had already told us. Peach was just being a

Tiny Brain!!

SUCK-UP!

Anyway, I would make a MUCH better therapy dog handler than Peach. Peach doesn't even have any dogs at home. Whereas I have Bob* who I have to handle ALL THE TIME on a daily basis.

handle!

FOOD

BOB

Licky Icky
DOG spit

* Bob is a very large, very licky golden retriever who needs LOTS of expert handling to keep him out of sticky situations.

Effie chose a couple of kids to have a turn at holding Charlie.** Nobody wanted to pat Eric the spider though. Not even "all-animals-loving" Peach. (Unfortunately.)

** Even though Effie must be really smart, because she studies reptiles and amphibians for her job, choosing Will Ashburner to hold a snake was a VERY BAD idea. Ms. Weiss asked Will to describe to everyone what Charlie's skin felt like and he said it was all slithery and slimy. And then Ms. Weiss said, "Are you sure? Snakes don't have slimy skin." And then Will said, "But it is slimy, Miss. Why is it slimy? Is it peeing on me???"

WILL ASHburner

EWW!

After all the animal experts had finished their talks Ms. Weiss asked if anyone in our class wanted to work with animals when we grow up.

Four people put up their hands.

 Me (of course!!).

 Cordelia (who is CRAZY about wombats).

3 Gavin (except he doesn't count, as he was just asking if he could go to the bathroom).

4 Sucky old Princess Peach (who probably just put her hand up because she likes getting attention).

ATTENTION seeker

And then we were allowed to ask one question each.

Cordelia asked how long wombats live for. And the answer was from five years to over thirty! She was really happy about that, especially when Angus let her hold darling Wally and feed him his bottle. Everyone was really jealous, especially You Know Who.

And then I asked if there was anything I could start doing now to help me get a job with animals when I finish school. And then Peach called out, in this really dramatic, sucky, whiny voice: "Yes, I want to know the answer to that too, please, because I am DESPERATE about working with animals. Animals are MY LIFE! And I want to make all the endangered animals un-endangered again."

Precious PEACH Parker

I ♥ animals.

And then all the animal experts turned away from me and smiled at Peach in this sick-making way instead. It made me

Soooo MAD!

And then they said to Peach that the best way was to start studying all about different animals now, while she was still at school. And a good way to do this was to choose an animal she liked and write a Fact File about it with stuff about its size and behavior and its natural habitat (which is the fancy scientific word for where animals live in the wild).

☑ SIZE.....

☑ Behavior....

☑ HABITAT.....

Peach smiled this really fake smile and said, "Ooo, what a good idea. Thank you! I'm going to start RIGHT AWAY."

← Fake
SMILE

And the animal experts all smiled back and said how wonderful it was to see young people today being so PASSIONATE about something they really cared about.

And then Ms. Weiss said she was going to award Peach a special Student Star for showing such "dedication and commitment." Which made her big fake smile grow even bigger and faker.

WAAAAAAHHHHHH!
Sometimes Peach makes me
so mad I want to throw up!

I bet she won't even write
any Fact Files. But *I'm* going
to. Because I *am* passionate about animals.
In fact, I'm going to start RIGHT NOW.

Because, fortunately, as you know, we have
a very large animal that I like a lot living
right here in this house. I'm going into the
kitchen (his natural habitat) right now to
find him.

See you later, Diary!

Friday night, before bed

Dear Diary,

Here is the FACT FILE I've started on Bob.

ANIMAL FACT FILE #①

BOB

Name: Bob.
Breed: Golden retriever.*
Color: Golden.
Coat: Long and shaggy
(except for the bit near his
ear where my little brother,
Max, tried to give him a haircut
with his safety scissors).

Age: Four and a half.

Weight: A LOT (especially when he sits on top of you when you are lying on the floor watching TV).

Appetite: Humungous to the power of 10.

Best habit: Licking you all over (it makes me laugh!).

Worst habit: Doing GINORMOUS stinky poops that I have to pick up in a special plastic doggie bag when I take him for walks each day.

* Retrieve means "to fetch something and bring it back." The things Bob most likes to retrieve are:

 1. The clothes off the line.

 2. Dad's slippers.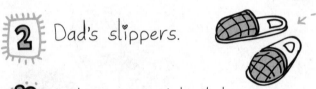

Dad's SLippers

3. Bits of food left lying around unguarded (especially CHEESE).

Although, actually, once he's retrieved any of these things he usually just eats them (or rips them up into little pieces).

This is fun! But just in case Peach does start writing a Fact File on some animal, I need to do some more so Ms. Weiss and everyone else can see I am even more dedicated and passionate than her. Which means I need MORE ANIMALS to study.

Tomorrow I'm going to ask Mom and Dad if we can get some more pets as a matter of

URGENT PRIORITY!

Good night, dearest Diary. Wish me luck!
XOXO

Saturday night, just before lights-out

Dear Diary,

I started off my "More Pets" campaign first thing by asking Dad if he could help me make pancakes for breakfast.

Mom LOVES pancakes. I figured this would put her in a good mood. And I've noticed that when Mom is in a good mood, Dad is in a good mood too. And when people are in a good mood, they are more likely to agree with your plans.*

* Unless your plans involve something really silly, like wanting to move to the North Pole

so it can be Christmas Day every day, or your own private jet to take you to school. Although imagine how aMAZing it would be if it was Christmas Day every day!!

Here's what happened:

Maple Syrup

Me (sweetly): More maple syrup on your pancakes, Mom?

Mom (suspiciously): Thank you, Ella. Have you been using my hairdryer again?

Me (shocked): No. Why would you think that?
Mom (winking at Dad): No reason.

Why do mothers always suspect you have
done something wrong if you do something
nice for them? I had another try.

Me: Mom?

BOB

Mom: Yes, Ella.
Me: Can we get some pets, please?
Mom: But we already have Bob.
Olivia (sneaking Bob some of her pancake
under the table): Bob's the best.
Max (holding his arms out wide):
I LOVE Bob up to the sky.

Me: I love Bob too. But I know everything about him already. I need more pets to study so I can be an animal expert when I grow up. Ple-e-e-ase can we get more pets? A fluffy bunny maybe? Or a cute little kitten? How about a guinea pig? Dad? What do you think?

Dad: No.

Me: Pretty please? I'll make

fluffy BUNNY

cute
Kitten

Guinea PIG

more pancakes. All by myself this time.
Mom and Dad, together:

Even though I used all my ESPOP (Ella's
Secret Powers of Persuasion) I could not get
my parents to change their minds.

ELLA'S SECRET POWERS OF Persuasion:

1 Offer to take the (stinky) trash cans out on trash day. Bleuchhh.

Stinky TRASH CAN!

2 Eat ALL of my broccoli without complaining. Double bleuchhh.

BROCCOLI

3 Be nice to Olivia by sharing my gel and glitter pens with her whenever she asks.

Glitter GEL Pens

Even when I reminded Mom and Dad that other types of pets wouldn't eat nearly as much as Bob, or retrieve the laundry, they still said no.

As soon as dinner was over I called Zoe. Zoe is EXTRA GOOD at coming up with helpful plans and schemes for getting your parents to do what you want them to.

ZOE'S HOUSE

MY HOUSE

I told her EVERYTHING that had happened.
Zoe thought for a bit. Then she said maybe
the reason Mom and Dad won't let me
get any more pets is because the ones I
suggested—like bunnies and kittens—are
just too plain and boring. This is because
Mom is a graphic designer and SUPER
STYLISH (like me). In fact, everything in
our house is stylish.

YEEEEEESSSSSSSSS! This must be the
reason!

So tomorrow I'm going to get up super
early and look up unusual and stylish pets
on Mom's computer.

SUPER · STYLISH · PETS

Never fear, dear Diary.

I.

    Will.

        Not.

           Give.

               Up.

E xx

Sunday morning, before breakfast

Hey, Diary,

There are HEAPS of stylish and unusual pets to choose from. Here's a list I made of the best ones:

MY TOP 5 stylish AND unusual PETS!

1 A lykoi (a type of cat that looks like a **Werewolf cat** ö).

 An *Idolomantis diabolica* **Praying Mantis** (a really cool-looking type of praying mantis).

cool-looking

 A **MADAGASCAR Hissing COCKROACH**.

hisssssss...

 A pygmy goat.

Pygmy GOAT

 An axolotl (also known as a Mexican walking fish).

Mexican walking FISH

Now all I have to do is ask Mom and Dad to let me get one of each of these fabulously fabulous pets, so I can start studying them in earnest. I just know they're going to say yes this time. Who wouldn't want to share their house with a werewolf cat, a teensy tiny sweet little miniature goat or a fish you can take for a walk?

Zoe is a GENIUS! I CAN'T WAIT TO GET STARTED!

Sunday morning, after breakfast

Mom and Dad still said no (especially when I showed them the photo of the hissing cockroach).

Sunday afternoon, before lunch

It is SO not fair that my parents won't let me get any more pets. Even plain and unstylish ones like cats or bunnies. Can't they see they are RUINING MY LIFE?

I decided to write a poem about it.

Cats purr
when you pat
and stroke them.
-- They sound just like --
a steam engine.
puuuuurrrrrrrr
They have twitchy
tails and they love chasing
moths and toys and running
up and down the hallway and also
climbing trees to the very top but they
do NOT like water. They love curling
up into a ball and snoozing in the
sun and they love snuggling
up close on your lap when
you're watching TV or
reading a book.
I wish I had a cat.

Then I decorated my poem with my best gel and glitter pens and stuck it to the fridge door. Now every time Mom and Dad get something out of the fridge, my poem will STARE back at them and they will know just how SERIOUS I am about my quest.

Sunday afternoon, after lunch

They still said no. ☹

Sunday, before dinner

Dearest Diary,

☑ SIZE .....
☑ Behavior ....

☑ HABITAT .....

I need to get more pets
to create more Fact Files or I will never get
a job with animals when I'm a grown-up. ☹

So I called Zoe and asked her to come over
for an EMERGENCY MEETING.

I put a new sign up on the door of my
bedroom to keep Olivia out, in case she
tried to annoy us by asking silly little girl
questions all the time.

KEEP OUT

EMERGENCY O.N.M.P. MEETING
NO little sisters
~~ALOUD~~ allowed

* O.N.M.P. stands for Operation Need More Pets

Then Zoe and I snuggled up on the bed with Bob (making sure none of our snacks were left unguarded) and discussed important P.A.S. (Pet-Acquiring Strategies).

YUM!

PET-ACQUIRING STRATEGIES AND REASONS WHY THEY WON'T SUCCEED

P.A.S. #1	REASONS WHY NOT
Smuggling new pets into my room and keeping them under my bed	Bob is sure to sniff them out or even try to retrieve them!
P.A.S. #2	REASONS WHY NOT
Keeping the new pets at Zoe's house instead ZOE'S HOUSE →	Her mom reckons she is allergic to all animals (although I think this might actually be a fib) Achoo...

Everything was looking horrendously hopelessly hopeless. ☹☹☹☹

We sat there sadly . . . like sad, sad-eyed kittens locked up in a cold, dark room, with no toys or bits of ribbon to pounce on or loving owners to give them cuddles . . . hoping for a happy solution to our sad problem.

sad-eyed kitten

Then Zoe said, "Something's scratching at the door."

And I said, "It's probably just Bob, trying to get out."

And Zoe said, "No, it's coming from OUTSIDE the door."

And I said, "Maybe it's a rat!" And then I got all excited because if it was a rat, I could maybe (secretly) keep it as a pet and write a Fact File about it.

But then the door opened. It wasn't a rat.

Squeak

RAT!

It was Olivia.

This is what she said: "Mom says you have to babysit Max and me in here for a bit."

She probably just made up the bit about Mom wanting us to babysit her and Max so she could come into my room. But I didn't care. Because as soon as she said the word "babysit" Zoe and I both had THE SAME BRILLIANT IDEA at EXACTLY THE SAME TIME! (Which is why we are BFFs.)

I'll have to write the next exciting installment later, Diary. Dad's calling me for dinner!

C U soon!

Sunday night, just before lights-out

OK, I'm back. I bet you're BUSTING to know what our brilliant idea was.

OK, here it comes.

Are you ready?

It's . . .

PET-sitting! Ta-daa!

Thanks, Olivia!

You know, for when people get sick or go away on vacation and have to leave their pets behind. Zoe and I could look after them! And while they were staying here, I could write Fact Files on them.

I was so excited, I told Mom and Dad ALL ABOUT IT at dinner.

The bad news

Mom and Dad said no way.
WAAAAAAHHHHHH!!!

The good news

Mom suggested we set up a pet-walking service instead. She reckons there are lots of pets around here who look like they don't get enough exercise. ~~Exspec~~ Especially George, the dog that lives across the street from us. Which is true. He's a real jelly belly. That way we could still be around pets without them being in our house.

JeLLY BELLY

So that's what I'm going to do. And while I'm walking the pets, I'm going to study them. I am going to be the Most Expert Expert in the History of Experts. (And Ms. Weiss will have to give me so many Student Stars there will be none left for Princess Peach to earn EVER AGAIN. Yay!)

STUDENT STARS

Monday, after school

Hey there, Diary,

I couldn't wait to get to school today so Zoe and I could discuss more details about our new pet-walking business. Ms. Weiss had to ask us THREE TIMES to stop talking when we should have been working.

And Peach kept looking over at our table and flapping her big ears, trying to hear what we were talking about.

BLEUCHHH!

NO WAY did we want
her to find out about our
excellent new business plans,
so we Z-I-I-I-PPPed our
mouths shut super-duper

zipped

MOUTH

tight. But it was really, really hard to keep
quiet. So many splendidly spectacular ideas
kept bubbling up into my head.

Like 1) what we were going to call our
business,

And 2) how much we were going to charge
per pet to walk them,

And 3) whether we should charge more for ferociously fierce pets (like Mr. Lau's Rottweiler, Zeus) than sweet and fluffy ones (like Mrs. Gatto's rabbit, Flopsy).*

* Though I'm not 100% sure that rabbits actually ever get taken for walks. It would be fun though!

...rabbit walking...

At lunchtime, we asked Ms. Weiss if we could borrow some materials from the arts and crafts cupboard. We explained we were setting up a pet-walking business and needed to make posters for it. And we said we were super sorry for talking in class so much but we were

SUPER EXCITED

about our plans and ideas kept bubbling

UP

UP

UP

and we just couldn't help ourselves.

And guess what? Ms. Weiss was really thrilled! She said she LOVES it when young people show ~~inishative~~ initiative** about stuff like this. She even said if she lived closer to my house and actually had a pet, she would be our first customer for sure.

So she helped us find all the stuff we needed:

Glitter ✭

Glue

Sheets OF COLORED poster board

marker PENS

STAR stickers

Scissors

and then she went off to the teachers' lounge while we made our posters.

** Showing initiative means you are good at getting something started all by yourself, without someone telling you what to do. Ms. Weiss is always using big words like that. The inside of her brain must be aMAZing.

enthralling

astonishing

mesmerizing

fascinating

awesome

awe-inspiring

captivating

→ Brain !!

Ms. Weiss

Are your pets bored?
Too tired to walk them or play with
them yourself?
Contact Zoe and Ella's Excellent
Pet-walking Service
on 5555 1252
for Sensational Service and
Reasonable Rates

I can't wait until we get our first customer!

Tuesday, just before dinner

Hey there, Diary,

Zoe came over to my place after school so we could put the posters up at the library and the local stores, like Choppers Hair Salon and Con's Meats.

Then we went home and sat in my bedroom, waiting for the phone to ring. This was it! Our big chance to be successful business SUPERSTARS!!!

Nobody called. ☹

After about 900 hours of sitting, Mom poked her head around the door and said there was a boy waiting to see us in the family room!

900 HRS

YES!!! Our very first customer!

Zoe and I ~~raced~~ strolled into the family room (so we didn't look TOO desperate, even if we ~~acksh~~ actually were). It was Henry Bing, a high school boy who lives at the end of our street.

Henry was carrying a large cardboard box.

"This is Lizzie," he said, pointing to the box.

Zoe and I gave each other a funny look. Did Henry want us to take a box for a walk? And why had he given his box a name? And how had he even known to come here? We didn't put my address on the poster.

Henry was *weird*. I was just about to say, "No, thank you very much, we're all full for today," when Henry opened the box. Zoe took a quick peek inside.

"Snake!" she screamed, jumping up on the sofa.

Henry reached into the box and pulled out a blue-tongue lizard. The lizard scampered up onto his shoulder and licked Henry under the chin with its tongue.

Zoe stopped screaming and climbed back down from the sofa again. I asked Henry why he'd come here and he said he'd seen me walking Bob in the park and chatting to other people about their pets and could tell I was a TRUE ANIMAL LOVER.

ZOW-EE! (So there, Peach. I wish all those animal experts were here right now so they could hear Henry call me that.)

Lizzie

Blue Tongue

Henry hadn't even seen our poster! He said he had important exams coming up next week so he didn't have enough time to look after Lizzie. And then he offered me ten dollars if I looked after her until his exams were finished because no one else in his family likes lizards very much. (Except for their cat Felix, who likes her so much he wants to eat her.)

Lizzie

Felix

But I had to promise,
cross our hearts hope
to die, to play with
her. And under NO
CIRCUMSTANCES to
let her go outside.

NO to OUTSIDE

Ten whole dollars! Plus a new species of
animal to study and write Fact Files about!
I was going to say yes straightaway, but then
I remembered what Mom and Dad had said.

NO PET-SITTING.

But Lizzie was so sweet! I was DESPERATE to look after her. And if Henry Bing thought I was a true animal lover, I needed another animal to love.

So I went and had a quick chat with Mom. After A LOT of begging and pleading from me, she finally said yes. On

STRICT CONDITIONS :

 I have to keep Lizzie in my room.

 I have to clean up Lizzie's mess and make sure she has food and clean water.

3 I have to stack and empty the dishwasher and set the table every night for three weeks WITHOUT COMPLAINING.

4 I have to promise, cross my heart hope to die, that I will NOT ask if I can look after any other pets.

So of course I said YES to everything, and it was all settled.

PHEWWWW!

Henry went home again and came back a few minutes later with the glass tank he keeps Lizzie in. It has a lightbulb up at one end to help keep her warm. Henry told us about all the things she likes to eat (slugs and snails mainly— bleuchhh), the best places to find these in the garden (double bleuchhh) and all her favorite games.

Have to go now, Diary. We're having pizza for dinner and I don't want to miss out!

Tuesday, after dinner

Dear Diary,

I am in the BIGGEST trouble. Henry's not going to speak to me EVER AGAIN. And Mom is REALLY, REALLY cross with me. She says I have LET HER DOWN. ☹

You know how I said we were having pizza for dinner? It was my favorite type—ham and pineapple with double extra cheese. I guess it must have been Lizzie's favorite type too.

MOM

YUM!

PIZZA

Anyway, after dinner, I was lifting Lizzie out of her fish tank so I could play with her. She must have smelled the pizza on my fingers because she started licking them with her bright-blue tongue. Then she BIT one with her hard little teeth.

I jumped about a mile and Lizzie escaped! She ran out of my room and made a bee-line for the back door, just as Dad was coming back inside from putting out the trash cans.

I ran straight into the backyard to look for her. Mom and Dad came out with flashlights and Olivia and Max and I called her and called her, but she didn't come back.

It's not looking good, Diary.
😣😣😣

Either Tuesday night, very, very late OR Wednesday morning, very, very early (I am too desperately upset to tell the difference)

Dearest Diary,

I just woke up from a horrifyingly horrible dream. A shaggy monster with golden fur had chased a sweet little dinosaur under a bush and was covering it with icky sticky slime that dripped from its ferocious fangs.

icky
sticky
SLIME

sweet
LITTLE
DinosauR

Then this gigantic
giant towered above
me and boomed, in
this extremely deep,
boomy voice, "It's all
your fault, Ella!"
What do you think it means?

It's all your
fault,
ELLA!

Wednesday morning, before breakfast

Dear Diary,

As soon as I woke up again, I went out into
the backyard to look for Lizzie. I called

her and called her but she didn't come.*
However I *did* discover a very nice-looking
praying mantis on a plant near the back
steps. I scooped him up and put him in
Lizzie's tank (along with some extra grass
and leaves) just in case Henry is tired of
lizards and decides
that a praying
mantis is the type
of pet he's really
wanted all along.

praying
mantis

* Maybe Lizzie doesn't have very good
hearing? In which case Henry should have
warned me about this. Bob ALWAYS

comes when he is called, especially if you are holding a cookie.

Wednesday, after school

Dear Diary,

I checked our backyard again as soon as I got home but Lizzie is still missing. I wonder if hide-and-seek is one of the games Lizzie likes to play? If so, she is

very, very good at it. Much better than Bob
and Max. Whenever I play hide-and-seek with
either of them, it
takes me about
4.392878625 seconds
to find them.

Next, I went inside
to find out if any
customers had
called. They hadn't.

Running a business can be VERY
disappointing. I don't know why grown-up
people even bother.

Thursday night, in bed, just before lights-out

Dearest Diary,

The Good News

I FOUND LIZZIE!!!

MR. SUPRAMANIAM

The Bad News

Actually, it was Mr. Supramaniam from next door who found Lizzie.

Accidentally.

And now I am in BIG TROUBLE again.

It was like this. Mr. Supramaniam came over to our place to borrow a ladder so he could trim his hedge, just as Mom was about to go into town for an important meeting.

And he was walking up the path that leads from the front gate to our front door when he (almost) stood on something.

FRONT DOOR

FRONT GATE

The something was Lizzie, who had crawled out of her hiding place in the garden and was sunning herself on our path.

"Snake!" screamed Mr. Supramaniam. Just like Zoe. Couldn't either of them see that Lizzie has LEGS????

Mom came running outside and spotted Lizzie on the path. She scooped her up so she could bring her safely back inside again.

The ~~Badder~~ Worse News

Mr. Supramaniam went white and started clutching his chest and told Mom he thought he was going to have a heart attack! Mom had to take him next door and help him find his heart pills and make sure he was OK.

Heart PILLS

And you know what that means, don't you?

She missed her important meeting.

☹

Nobody said anything bad to me when I came home from school but I could tell by their faces exactly what they were all thinking:

"Ella is a Troublemaker. With a capital T."

See, Diary? Just like in my horrifying nightmare, it was ALL MY FAULT.

ME

Mr. Supramaniam

MOM

Thursday night, a few minutes after I last wrote to you

Oh yeah. I forgot to say.

Still no customers.

Thursday night, a few more minutes after that

I can't get to sleep. Not even when I try counting sheep. So I'm going to write a Fact File on Lizzie instead.

ANIMAL ⚬ FACT FILE #②

Name: Lizzie.

Breed: Eastern blue-tongue lizard.

Color: Gray with brown stripes on her back and tail.

Body shape: A big head and long body with a fat tail, extremely short legs and little feet.

Distinguishing feature: A bright-blue tongue inside a pink mouth (plus extremely hard teeth that

Lizzie

Short Legs

LITTLE FEET

BRIGHT-Blue Tongue

chomp down on your finger if it smells like pizza).

Why her tongue is blue: To scare predators so they won't gobble her up. If an enemy tries to attack her, she sticks her tongue out at them.

Why she likes sleeping on paths in the sunshine: Because she is cold-blooded and the sun helps to warm up her body so she can move around better.

G'night, Diary. I think I'm starting to get sleepy now.

Friday, after school

Dear Diary,

Princess Peach has been acting very suspiciously lately. She is definitely up to something super sneaky.

So sneaky I've decided to start an Evidence Fact File on her. I've been watching her really, really closely, just like I do when I'm writing my Animal Fact Files. But even the sneakiest animal—like a fox or a weaselly weasel—could NEVER be as sneaky as Precious Peach Parker. Here's what I've found out so far . . .

EVIDENCE FACT FILE #①

Today at school when Ms. Weiss asked Zoe and me how our pet-walking business was going, Peach and her friends Prinny and Jade were listening in with big sneery smirks on their faces, like they know something I don't know. Then afterward, they kept looking over at Zoe and me and whispering and giggling like maniacs.

NORMAL SMILE

SNEERY SMIRK

SUSPicious Behavior RATING: 7

EVIDENCE FACT file #: 2

At lunchtime, Zoe and I were standing behind
Peach and her friends in the cafeteria line.
They were spending big on snacks and
treats. They even bought drinks and ice
cream and gave them out to other girls in
our grade, like Grace and Lily.

Peach doesn't even LIKE Grace and Lily.

SUSPICIOUS Behavior RATING: 5

Stay tuned for more evidence from my
SBEF (Suspicious Behavior Evidence File).

Friday night, just before bedtime

Dear Diary,

Lizzie and I had a lovely time this evening snuggled up together on the sofa. We were watching a movie about a family that raises a baby lion cub after its mother is killed by hunters. When the baby lion cub grows up they release it back into the wild, so it can be free to be its lion self. That is just SO adorable!

mommy
↙ LiON

At the end of the movie, they find the lion again and it has had three babies.

I wish I had one of those babies, Diary. I would take EXTRA special care of it.

xOxO

BaBY Lions

Saturday morning, just before lunch

Zoe just called me to say she was coming back from the store with her mom and when they were driving along Calico Drive she saw Peach coming out of her front gate with lots of dogs on leashes. She said they were heading for Calico Park.

WHAAAAATTTTTTT!!!

Peach ✚ dog on leash ✚ Calico Park ≡ Extremely SUSPICIOUS BEHAVIOR

I told Zoe to ask her mom if she could come over IMMEDIATELY for an

Stay tuned!

Saturday night, before dinner

Dearest Diary,

There is so much to tell you! As soon as Zoe arrived we raced down to Calico Park to see if we could find Peach and her pooches.

It didn't take long. We saw her over near the fountain with five dogs on leashes. In BROAD DAYLIGHT!

How DARE she!

Zoe and I were SHOCKED.

This is what we said to each other:

Me: I'm SHOCKED!
Zoe: Same.
Me: How DARE she!
Zoe: That is just SO

like Peach. Stealing
our idea.
Me: I know. Look at her. She's not even
trying to hide the fact that she's stolen our
idea.
Zoe: What are we going to do about it?
Me: We're going to go over to her RIGHT
NOW and ask her what's going on.
Zoe: Bring it on!

So we walked right up to her and asked her.
This is how the next bit went:

Me (hands on hips): Hi, Peach. What
are you doing?
Peach (smiling fakely): Hi, Ella. Hi,
Zoe. What are you doing?
Me: I asked you first.
Peach: I asked you second.
Me: That doesn't even make sense.
Come on. What are you doing?
Peach: Walking these dogs. What
does it look like I'm doing?
Zoe: Stop being such a
smarty-pants, Peach. You
know what we mean.

And then Peach told us the dogs belonged
to her aunt who had gone away on vacation
to Timbuktooty. Which I bet is a big fib.
Who has five dogs that don't even look
like each other? And
I bet there's not even
a real place called
Timbuktooty. She
probably just made
that up.

Timbuktooty

So I said, "You've started up your own pet-
walking business, haven't you? You are such
a COPYCAT."

And then Peach said, "Prove it."

And then she just laughed IN MY FACE and walked away.

Ha! ha Ha

Peach

Grrrrrrr!

Sometimes, Diary, Peach makes me SO MAD!

This means WAR!

Me

MAD

Saturday night, before bed

Dear Diary,

I cannot BELIEVE that Princess Peach could be so mean.

Yes, I can. Peach is ALWAYS mean. She is the QUEEN of mean!

QUEEN OF mean

This explains all the smirky looks she's been giving me lately. And the extra cash to spend in the cafeteria.

But where, Diary? Where is she getting all her customers from?

And how come Zoe and I still don't have any? Our posters have been up for FIVE WHOLE DAYS and so far our only customer has been Henry Bing (who doesn't even count).

It is all a BIG MYSTERY, Diary. And there is only one way to solve it.

We need to collect MORE EVIDENCE.

XOXO

Sunday, before lunch

Dear Diary,

Zoe came over this morning for another Emergency Meeting. Max and I were out in the garden when she arrived, collecting slugs and snails (eww) from under rocks for Lizzie's lunch. (Lizzie LOVES lunch. I hope I am not overfeeding her though as she seems to be getting a bit chubby.)

MAX

Zoe and I decided the best way to collect more evidence on Peach was to stake out* her house. That way we could check to see if . . .

(A) the dogs really *did* belong to her aunt or . . .

(B) they were being dropped off by her (who should be our!!!) customers.

* Staking out means keeping a close watch on something from the other side of the street.

There was only one snag with our plan.
How were we going to stake out her house
without her noticing we were there?

So we thought up some sneaky ways.

SNEAKY WAYS TO STAKE OUT PEACH'S HOUSE AND CHANCE OF THEM WORKING

SNEAKY WAY	CHANCE	REASON WHY
Disguise ourselves as trees by sticking leaves and branches all over ourselves	0%	Anyone with even a tiny brain would be able to tell we weren't trees straightaway

Disguise ourselves as gas meter readers	0% 	We didn't have any gas meter reader uniforms, and even if we did they would be too big for us
Get invisibility cloaks (real ones)	0%	I'm not 100% sure these are actually real

As you can see, Diary, things were NOT LOOKING GOOD.

Then I remembered that Cordelia, from our class, lives DIRECTLY OPPOSITE Peach's house.

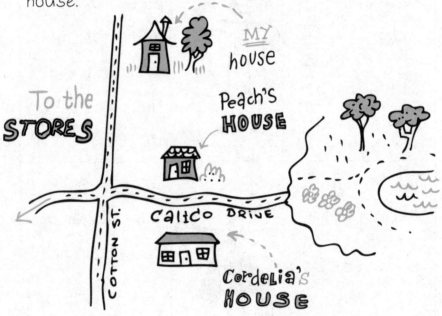

Cordelia has never trusted Peach, ever since she tried to make me kidnap and hide Mr. Wombat, Cordelia's favorite toy. So I KNEW she'd be on our side. But she is

also VERY GOOD at noticing things.
And guess what?! When we called her and
asked if she'd seen anything extremely
suspicious, she said
people had been
dropping dogs off at
Peach's house all week!

MR. Wombat

YES!

So then Zoe and I worked out another plan.
A Super-Duper Grand Kabuper one.

We're going to put it into action after lunch!

Stay even more tuned!

Sunday night, before dinner

There is sooo much to tell you, Diary!
At exactly 2:32 pm, four TOP-SECRET
DETECTIVES trooped off to the park,
dressed in our stylish and practical TOP-
SECRET DETECTIVE outfits (selected
by me).

This is who went: THE fearless FOUR

TSD #1: ME

COMBAT
STRIPES
n FACE

BINOCULARS

TSD #2: ZOE

NoteBook

soft-SOLed SHOES

TSD #3: CORDELIA
(and Mr. Wombat)

IDENTITY-hiding SunGLasses

DARK JEANS --->

MR. WOMBAT

GREEN T-SHIRTS

TSD #4: BOB

pencil
(For jotting down EVIDENCE)

We all hid behind a big tree and waited for Peach to turn up.

After about 900 hours of waiting, I finally spotted Peach walking into the park with six dogs on leashes. And guess what? One of them was George, the jelly belly from across the street!

GEORGE

A couple of seconds later, Prinny and Jade turned up.

Big surprise (not).

They spent a few minutes telling each other how fabulously fabulous they were all looking. Bleuchhh.

Then Peach gave her friends two dogs each and they all started walking them around the park, chatting away chattily.

So it's true. Princess Peach HAS set up her own dog-walking business!

How DARE she!!!

I quickly jotted down some notes in my Evidence Fact File then used secret hand signals to secretly signal to the others: MISSION ACCOMPLISHED.

TIME TO LEAVE.

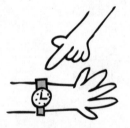

Just at that moment, a bird swooped down out of the tree, right in front of Bob's nose. Then it swooped across the park, daring Bob to chase it.

Bob loves chasing birds almost as much as he loves cookies (which is A LOT). He broke free and chased after the bird.

And then . . .

da da da DUMMMM . . .

he saw Peach and the two fluffy miniature poodles she was walking.

NOOOOOOOOOOOOOOO!!!

Bob loves chasing poodles even more than he loves chasing birds. (Though not as much as cookies.) He took off after them.

When the poodles saw Bob coming, they took off too, dragging Peach with them. They all went through a giant mud puddle

and across the fountain

and through the prickly prickle bushes

and between the swings

and ALMOST through the middle of a picnic. Fortunately Bob stopped here because he could smell egg-and-bacon pie and other yummy smells, and Peach and her pooches managed to escape.

I had to creep commando-style on my hands and knees through the bushes (and mud puddles) to retrieve him, in case Peach and her friends looked back and saw me.

MUD PUDDLE

Then Bob and I returned to our tree and we all ran away quickly.

Being a Top-Secret Detective is HARD WORK!

Sunday night, just before lights-out

Dear Diary,

Princess Peach probably thinks she is sooo clever, stealing all my customers. I am not 100% sure how she did it yet, but I have a PLAN.

> Good night
> Sleep tight
> Won't give up
> without a fight.

PS Lizzie looks even fatter today. I'm going to cut out some of her snails and give her some nice slimming lettuce and broccoli instead.

BiG FAT
TUMMY

Monday, before dinner

Dearest Diary,

So today I put my plan into action. You will NOT BELIEVE what I found out!!

Remember how I said one of the dogs Peach was walking yesterday was George, from across the street? Well, straight after school I put Bob on his leash but instead of going to the park I took him over to see George's owner, Mavis.＊

* Mavis is this really sweet little old lady with permed blue hair who's about 800 years old. She and Nanna Kate's nanna probably went to kindergarten together.

Here is a small part of what we said: (Mavis likes to talk. A LOT.)

Mavis: Would you like another homemade cookie, dear?

Me (politely): Yes, please. Can I have one for Bob too? Bob LOVES cookies.

Bob: Crunch, crunch, crunch.

Mavis: So what exactly did you want to talk to me about, Elspeth?

CRUNCH

Me: Ella.

Mavis: Pardon, dear?

Me: Ella. My name is Ella.

Mavis: Helen. What a lovely name!

Me (moving really, really close to Mavis so she can hear me better): I saw George at the park yesterday. With a *girl*.

Mavis: Yes! He *loved* his walk with that lovely girl. I was so lucky I saw that poster at Choppers.

Me (choking on my orangeade):

There was *heaps* more but I can hear Lizzie scrabbling around in her glass tank which means she's probably hungry (again) so here are the main facts:

1 Mavis saw our poster at Choppers and thought, "What a good idea. I will get those nice girls to take dear George for a walk now that my poor old legs are too ancient and wobbly to do it myself."

ANCIENT and wobbly LEGS!

2 She called the number on the poster and a girl answered and said, "Why, yes,

YES!

I would love to take George for a walk and I will only charge you ten dollars a time."

3 I asked Mavis if she still had the number she called and she said, "Yes, I wrote it down somewhere, dear, oh here it is," and she showed it to me and it WASN'T EVEN MY NUMBER!

Guess whose number it was, dear Diary?

Hint: Her name rhymes  with "SCREECH."

I finally had evidence that Peach has stolen my pet-walking company from right under my nose!

But to be 150% sure, I needed to check the poster for myself. I called Zoe and asked her to meet me at Choppers as a matter of URGENT PRIORITY.

This is what we found:

Are your pets bored?
Too tired to walk them or play with them yourself?
Contact Zoe and Ella's Excellent Pet-walking Service
on ~~5555 4252~~ **5555 6848**
for Sensational Service and Reasonable Rates

Peach had crossed out my phone number and put hers in instead!

Next, we checked all the other posters we'd put up. Every single one had been changed. Even the one at the library!

WAAAAAAAAAHHHH!

Zoe and I have to stop Peach stealing our customers. But how exactly?

We need another plan.

Tuesday night, just before lights-out

Dear Diary,

I have to be really, really careful not to let Peach know that I know EXACTLY what she's been up to. Not till I've worked out how we're going to get all my customers back. I made Zoe promise, cross her heart hope to die, not to say anything either.

I promise.

← ZOE

So today, whenever Peach:

1 sneered one of her sneery smirks,

OR

2 talked to her friends in front of
me about all the fabulously fabulous
things they're going to buy at the local
shopping mall,

OR

3 asked me in a really fake voice how
my plans to become the world's most
expert animal expert were going . . .

I just ignored her.

Zow-ee. That REALLY made her mad.
Peach HATES being ignored.

Tuesday night, about ten minutes later

If I say the word PLAN six times really fast and then bang my head on the pillow, when I wake up in the morning a plan will have magically jumped into my brain.

Here goes.

PLAN
    PLAN
        PLAN
            PLAN
                PLAN

Wednesday morning, before breakfast

Still no plan. Maybe it was supposed to be seven times . . .

Wednesday, after dinner, when I'm supposed to be doing my math homework

Dearest Diary,

I have a new problem. I don't think Lizzie is very well.

She keeps making little nests among the grass and twigs in her tank, so she can lie down quietly in them. Just like Mom does when *she* isn't feeling very well. (Lie down quietly, I mean. Not make little nests in a tank.)

And even though I've been feeding Lizzie
heaps of slimming lettuce and broccoli, she
keeps getting fatter and fatter.

Henry Bing is going to be
REALLY cross with me
when he comes back to
pick her up and discovers
his sweet little lizard has
turned into **Godzilla**
while in my care.

GODZILLA
(Lizzie!)

And then I thought: Maybe Lizzie would
feel better if she had a little run around
outside in the fresh air. Plus it might help
her lose some weight! YES!

I got Max's old playpen out of the shed and set it up on the lawn, just in case Lizzie tried to escape again. (Or scare any other neighbors. Mr. Supramaniam STILL gives me worried looks every time I pass him in the street, in case I'm secretly planning to do something that will make his heart go all jumpy again.)

I needn't have worried though. Lizzie just lay there, like one of those pretend animal garden ornaments that people put in their gardens.

There were lots of other things moving around though.

THINGS I SAW MOVING AROUND IN OUR GARDEN

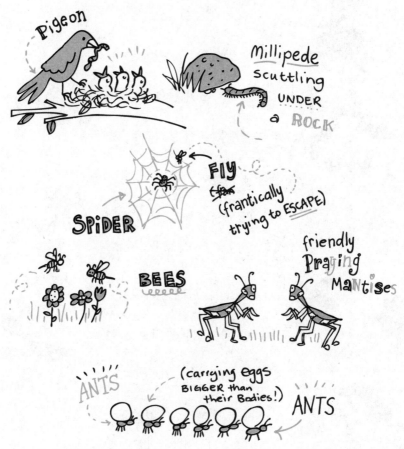

Pigeon

Millipede scuttling UNDER a ROCK

FLY ~~(far)~~ (frantically trying to ESCAPE)

SPIDER

BEES

friendly Praying MaNtises

ANTS (carrying eggs BIGGER than their Bodies!) ANTS

It was aMAZing!

So amazing, I wrote this poem about it.

Elegant spiders

Weaving webs

Lines of soldier ants

Carrying eggs

Wiggly, wriggly worms

And busy buzzy bees

Butterflies fluttering

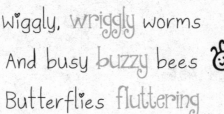

Through the trees

Praying mantises

Pigeons in nests

Visit your garden—

It's the best!

Thursday night, who cares what time exactly

I STILL couldn't think of a plan to get my customers back, so Zoe and I decided to have another Emergency Meeting in my room. I was SO DESPERATE, I even let Olivia come, in case she had any good ideas. (She didn't.)

We collected lots of snacks from the fridge and piled onto my bed (which meant there was no room for Bob, so he sat on the floor instead, looking wistfully at our food). Then we got down to our Very Important Business.

THE IDEAS WE CAME UP WITH AND THE REASONS WHY THEY WOULDN'T WORK

IDEA	REASONS WHY NOT
Do nothing OLiVia's ← REALLY DUMB { IDEA }	This idea is just silly and time wasting
Hope that Peach develops an allergy to animals, like Zoe's mom	So is this
Change all the phone numbers on the posters back to MY number	Peach will probably just change them all back again

Tell all the customers that Peach has Occhilupo's disease, which is highly contagious and deadly to animals, especially dogs

How would we ever find all the customers, and anyway, Occhilupo's disease is just something I made up once to get out of going to school. You can tell I'm getting REALLY desperate now

It's all hopelessly hopeless. Without any animals to study, I will never become a Top Animal Expert. Or be awarded any Student Stars by Ms. Weiss.

My life is over.

Good night, Diary. Sometimes I think you're the only one who cares.
XOXO

Saturday night, WAY past my bedtime (but I'm too excited to go to sleep)

Dearest, darlingest, bestest Diary in the whole wild world,

Guess what happened today?!!!!

I was on my way to the park with Bob for his daily walk and Mavis came out of her house and waved me over. She asked if I would mind taking George to the park for a walk too.

So of course I had to ask why "that lovely girl" wasn't taking him and Mavis said one of the dogs she walks had ringworm (eww). And then Peach got it too (ha!), because she didn't wash her hands properly after handling the dog. And now half of the rest of the dogs she walks have got yucky old ringworm as well.

Mavis says her friend Myrtle (who owns the miniature poodles) told her all about it while they were sitting next to each other getting their perms done at Choppers.

And NO WAY JOSÉ* does she want Peach
to keep walking George in case he gets it
too. Ringworm is HIGHLY CONTAGIOUS,
just like Occhilupo's disease would be if it
actually was a real disease.

Yay!!

* (Say José like this: HO-ZAY.)

Poor Peach. Maybe I should
send her a Get Well card. ☺

And guess what else?!!!

Henry came over to get Lizzie. When he bent down to pick her up out of the tank he went, "Oh, wow!"

And it wasn't because she was so fat. It was because she'd just had thirteen babies! (That's ten more babies than that lion cub from the movie that got released back into the wild.) They were all squirming around squirmishly in the tank beside her.

Henry said he'd wait till they were a bit bigger and then he'd release them into the wild as well. But here's the BEST bit. He said if I wanted, I could have one of Lizzie's babies! To keep forever and ever! So I picked out a really wriggly one that had a nice smile. I'm going to call her Iggy.

Iggy's going to stay with Henry until she's big enough to live on her own. But you know what? I'm not going to keep her in a tank. I'm going to let her live in the garden,** with all the other wild things, where she belongs.

** After I've trained Bob not to retrieve her, so there aren't any TRAGIC ACCIDENTS.

And guess what else?!!!

Even though Princess Peach ruined my pet-walking business, I can STILL be a Top Animal Expert after all.

There are a whole lot of interesting and amazing animals living RIGHT HERE IN MY GARDEN.

Beetles

And I'm going to write fabulously fabulous Fact Files on every one of them.

Starting tomorrow.

Love, Ella xox

grasshopper

PS (one week later)

Guess what?! Myrtle asked Mavis to ask me if Zoe and I could walk her two poodles, Fluffy and Trixibelle. You know, because of Peach and the RINGWORM.

Fluffy ♡ Trixibelle

And guess what else?!

The other dog owners want us to walk their dogs as well!

We could be rich business ~~magnets~~ magnates!

But you know what, Diary? Now that I've got Iggy and my wild things, two dogs is enough.

For now. ☺

See you!

PPS (two weeks later)

Peach's ringworm SPREAD. Now she has ringworm all over her arms and legs.

And then Prinny and Jade got it too.

Eww.

They're not allowed to come back to school until next term.

WOO HOO!

Love, Ella xOxO

Diaries

Read them all!